COLD STORAGE

A.K. MASON

Coldstorage is a work of fiction.
Names, characters, places and incidents are the
products of the author's imagination or are used
fictitiously. Any resemblance to actual events,
locales, or persons, living or dead,
is entirely coincidental.

Copyright © 2012 by A.K Mason
All rights reserved. No part of this book may be
used or reproduced in any form, electronic or
mechanical, including photocopying, recording, or
scanning into any information storage and retrieval
system, without written permission from the author
except in the case of brief quotation embodied
in critical articles and reviews.

Cover design by A.K. Mason

Printed in the United States of America

The Troy Book Makers • Troy, New York
thetroybookmakers.com

To order additional copies of this title, contact your
favorite local bookstore or visit www.tbmbooks.com

ISBN: 978-1-61468-194-6

DEDICATION

This is book is dedicated to my grandfather who passed away at 92 years of age or "Checked out" as he chose to put it approximately one hour from the time the last sentence of this book was written.

He never knew we were writing this. Gramp you will be greatly missed. I will give you a copy one day.

SPECIAL THANKS TO OUR LOCAL BUSINESSES

Spaulding Computers

The UPS Store, Guilderland

Jack's Oyster House

The Troy Book Makers

Book House of Stuyvesant Plaza

Sunmark Federal Credit Union

The Altamont Enterprise

AND OUR FAMILY

Mom's mother, my grandmother
And, most important, saving the best for last:
Our loving, tolerant husbands for putting up
with us unaware of what our mission was.

PROLOG

Saturday, May 2012

Feeling a cold damp sensation she slowly awakens to the sound of traffic, only to realize her eyes refuse to open. Smelling a musty fowl odor accompanied by a wicked headache she realizes she has been drugged.

She finally wills her eyes to open, shields her face with her hands until her eyes adjust to the bright light from the small window above. Her head feels like its about to explode. Confused as to how she got there, where she is, and why? She is more scared than she has ever been before in her life, and doesn't like the feeling.

Starting to panic, not knowing how to handle her new found situation, she tries to get to her feet, staggering as the nausea threatens to take hold. She soon realizes she is in a small tomb like room with one small window and one door, both with thick thermal metal closures. The door to the window is open, with only glass separating her from the outside world. The door to the room is bolted shut from the other side. She knows this is no accident. Rushing to look out the small window, staggering to catch her balance, looking out and realizing she is on at least the 10th floor, baffled to be looking down at Rte. 787.

She has no idea what time it is or how long she has been unconscious. It must be early morning with the sun just rising. All at once it hits her. She must have been here all night!

Looking around the room at the concrete walls and floor, they appear to be some form of old insulation. Being an Albany native born and raised in the city, her best guess is she is locked in Old Central Warehouse. But why?

How did she get here?

Looking down she notices all her jewelry is gone. Her wedding ring and her watch have been removed. She has no purse and no cell phone.

Who would do this?

Not seeing anyone on the ground, it wouldn't do any good to call for help. With the rush hour traffic and the height of the building, no one would hear anyway.

In one corner of the room near the door, someone left her four gallons of water, three loaves of bread, and an empty five gallon pail.

Chapter 1

I awoke at 5am to the sound of my alarm only to find that my king size bed was empty. It is usually occupied by myself and my boys as I call them. They would be Tuko & Boscarelli my 8&2 year old German Shepherds. My name is Julianna Angellotti. Yes, of Italian decent. My friends call me Jewels. I am 5'5" 35 years old, 123 lbs. and have brown hair, green eyes, and a mild attitude, or so I am told.

I am not at all thrilled with surprises and my good sense tells me I'm about to get one.

There are only two people in the world my boys love as much as me. One is my mom, "grammies", who they see and fuss over on a regular basis. The other, whom they hardly ever see but completely adore, is Ombre an ex-Navy seal and my best friend.

He is 40 years old, never been married, and has always lived life the most difficult way possible.

He's hard on a relationship, even harder on a friendship; but, I seem to be the only one to survive him. Having had both, I have more insight than others.

He is 6ft. 3in. tall and 300 lbs. of solid muscle and attitude. He is extremely over protective and pisses me off every chance he gets.

Since I smell coffee brewing, some form of breakfast cooking, and I haven't heard any security breach barking, I'm guessing Ombre is in my kitchen schmoosing my boys.

Every now and then he comes and goes like the wind. His Seal team gave him the nick name Ombre because it means shadow in Italian. They say that's where he lives, in the shadows. At least when he's not living at my place.

My place, by the way, is a cape style house, in a quiet neighborhood, just off Central Avenue. It is 1,000 sq. ft. of cozy bliss with an attached garage. My friends pick on me about the decor. I hate pastels and brightly colored rooms. I am, however, a big fan of earth tones and dark warm spaces. That and Ombre explains my love of camouflage as a teenager.

He has never had a key. Never needed one. I never hear him come or leave. The boys do but they never bark. They meet him at the door or window tails wagging.

Other than my dad, no man has ever made me breakfast before.

I stroll down stairs toward the aromas coming from my kitchen and am immediately greeted by the best bear hug you can imagine. There is no other like it.

"I've missed you" he whispers in my ear in that soft raspy voice I've heard on a few other occasions. "And, you smell good too."

"So does breakfast I added and I'm starving. For food that is."

Our eyes locked as he smirked at me the way only he can.

I felt a flutter and moved on toward the coffee pot. I've missed him too. I always do but rarely let him know that. It's just not wise.

As he put scrambled eggs and toast on the table with some fresh homemade jam he found in my fridge, he started talking as we ate.

"I need a little help if you have some free time."

I look at him and say, "Over the last 20 years you have always been there for me. You know if there is anything I can do to help you I will."

From which I got the smirk again.

"We don't have a lot of time for that right now

but I will definitely put it on my list for later" he said still smirking. "Some things can't be rushed."

"I need some help solving this case so I can clear my name," he said as he ate his eggs.

"I tell you what. You fill me in from the beginning, and mom and I will help you any way we can. But, I want the whole story start to finish, nothing left out. I know you hate to give information, almost as much as I hate surprises! I have to go to work today. How about we meet back here for dinner tonight with mom and hash it out?"

"Sounds like a plan. What's for dinner he asked?"

To which I replied, "You have all day to think about it. There is lots of food in the freezer. Build something! I'm going to go jump in the shower and get ready for work. How does 5:00 sound?"

"Works for me he said. I'll build something fabulous!"

"Great I'll tell mom and we'll meet you back here at 5:00."

"Cool. If you need any help in the shower just yell."

I shook off the idea and replied, "I think I can handle it", as I put my plate in the sink and trudged up stairs. On the way I yelled back "Feed the boys and thanks for breakfast."

"No problem."

Chapter 2

I'm usually at work by 7am to open my salon. It gives me time to set up my day, make some coffee, and read the local paper before my first appointment. If I have some extra time, I like to go over some evening case files before my usual Monday morning line up arrives.

My salon is on Central Avenue in Albany. It has a style all its own. And, like other aspects of my life, I like it warm and inviting, unlike most salons. No Bright Colors! With it's post&beam design, and large fireplace, on chilly days most clients come early to grab a cup of coffee by the fire. I don't do well in frilly-fufu spaces. I love the simple basic things in life.

By day I cut hair. I enjoy it and I like my clientele. They sure do keep life interesting.

For instance, my 89 year old Annie, an avid

reader of steamy romances says "I could have written them. I wasn't always old you know."

Annie's favorite things include: frozen mud slides, Milky Ways and books with large print.

By night I'm a licensed private investigator. That's when the real fun begins.

I work with my mom. Her name is Angeline Angellotti. She is 5`2, 57 years old and 102 pounds. She also has brown hair, green eyes (inherited from her father) and a mild attitude. She is a nurse by day and my partner in Soul Sisters Investigations at night. That apple didn't fall far from the tree.

We work very well together using very little conversation. It's the same brain hard at work. When we do speak, we finish each others sentences and ideas. We are both skilled marks women and trained by the best in self defense.

I left her a voice mail about dinner tonight. She usually checks her phone in between patients and calls me back.

Mom is a firm believer in the phrase bees with honey. She is one of those remarkable people who can be totally pissed off and smile the sweetest smile while always remaining calm and always getting what she wants. She refers to it as shmoozing and she can schmooze anyone into anything when she puts her mind to it. She just smiles and says "I got this", and it is done.

Everyone except my dad that is. He is the exception to all her rules. They say opposites attract. It appears to be true in this case. He marches to the beat of his own drum.

She doesn't have the same power over him. However, if she wants something badly enough, she gets it but, not without serious negotiation.

My dad, Joseph Angellotti, is 5'6" tall, 160 lbs., with a full head of salt and pepper wavy hair, light brown eyes, sometimes serine, sometimes short fused and built like a brick shit house.

Having grown up within a few blocks of each other and graduating together, at 17 years old dad enlisted in the Navy during the Vietnam War and Cuban Crisis of the 1960's. On leave after basic training in the Great Lakes, he came home to find his girlfriend had strayed.

At the time, mom worked at a grocery store on the corner of Central and Colvin Avenues.

Finishing her shift one summer evening, she found my dad leaning against her car in the parking lot waiting for her. And, that's where it all began.

They now live on a side street off Central Avenue, just around the corner from me and around another corner from my grandmother. None of us moved too far from our beginning. My parent's house, or the Angel's cloud as I call it, is a large three-story brownstone, built with sandstone, a once popular building material, mostly built in the late 1800s in rows, thus the term row houses. The 3,600 sq. ft. cloud includes a basement rental apartment with access beneath the ornate front staircase with wrought iron railings.

The rental business, however, has provided hours upon hours of live entertainment. I often joke that mom screens for drama when interviewing tenants. They even built a new composite deck out back for our summer amusement. Beneath it is the basement apartment patio where a constant steady flow of crazies reside.

Currently mom is interviewing a perspective tenant by the name of Damien O'Hiney, newly transferred to the hospital from New York City. "He seems like a very nice young man. I have high hopes for this one. He's an adorable, calm, happy go lucky Greek/Irish medical examiner with blonde hair, blue eyes, and a perky attitude."

Chapter 3

My phone rang around 11:30 am. I picked up to mom. "What's up missy?"

I said "My Ombre appeared. He needs a little help and wants to discuss it over dinner at my place tonight. You free?"

"That depends. What's for dinner?"

"I don't know yet. He says he is making something fabulous."

"I guess I'll enter at my own risk. What time?"

"I told him 5:00 because it's gym night. Do you want to meet me at the Lift & Pump at 4:00?"

"How about Fritzie's Pub at 3:30 mom suggested."

"I like it. I will see you then."

Mom and I work out on Monday, Wednesday and Friday around cocktails of course.

I whittled my way through my afternoon with a protein shake and some Monday afternoon standing appointments. I was thinking some days take longer to get through than others, when I came to the realization that it was 5:00 I was looking forward to.

On most days it was happy hour on the top of my list. I work all day for that ice cold glass of wine reward . Now I find myself thinking of other things I have done with ice in the past and that smirk of his comes creeping into my mind much to clearly.

I shook it out, locked my salon and headed down Central Avenue on foot. It was a beautiful spring day. The sun was shining. I strolled past my grandmother's bright yellow bungalow at a high rate of speed so as not to be detected because she always wants to go with us. Most days, any time of the day, she is sitting on her front porch with her drinks-a glass of water, a half glass of prune juice and her Chablis.

My grandmother at 75 years young believes she's a detective because it is in her blood along with lots of Chablis. Her father Anthony Audino, was detective/police chief in Albany years ago in the 1940's and 50's.

Getting past, undetected, not looking in Mancini's Bakery at the calories in the window I took a quick right into Fritzie's Pub.

Fritzie's Pub is famous for it's Irish fare which includes bangers & chips, shepard's pie and Gaelic grilled cheese.

The dimly lit pub, with it's dark timbers, handcrafted metal work fixtures is a combination of natural materials and artistic traditions. An oak carved bar with marble armrest railing and rows of polished brass taps. Wooden stools on wrought iron stands fixed to the floor sit on half stone, half wide plank boards scuffed by hundreds of pairs of shuffling shoes, reminiscent of old Irish ways. Adding to the warm atmosphere is a large open stone fireplace with a cast iron kettle. To the right of the bar is an antique claw foot piano and dance floor.

Mom was talking to our favorite bartender in the world, Jack Vogner. Jack is a portly, very happy go lucky man about 80 years young with a bit of a drinking problem and an IQ that is through the roof. He is always neatly dressed due to his military background, with his white T shirt, perfectly starched cream colored, long sleeved shirt, pressed khaki slacks, and brown polished shoes. He is exactly what you would want to see when you walk into a business.

Jack is one of our go to guys when we need information on a case. He knows everything, everyone and can find out almost anything just by paying unnoticed attention to bar conversation.

Mom has always had a soft spot for Jack because he reminds her of her dad, my gramp, who passed away some years ago. Sometimes the similarities are uncanny!

Jack flashes a bright smile at me as I walk toward the bar. With his round face and twinkly eyes, he is one of those people who always looks generally happy to see you.

When he starts to pour my signature glass of Chardonnay, I smile back at him and ask, "Please Jack hold the ice today."

Mom frowned at me and asked "Why? You always get ice".

"Not now I said, move along".

"Alrighty then" she says as she studies the expression on my face.

"I can't help but wonder if it's wise that he's staying at your place with your history and all."

I rolled my eyes at her.

"I'm just saying."

"I know what you are saying, but what am I supposed to do? He has always been there for me. I can't just kick him out."

"I know. I love him too, but I don't think its wise."

"Well maybe if we help him clear his name he will drift back into the shadows. He always has in the past." (Whether I want him to or not).

"You know I'm in she says. Finish your wine so we can hit the gym."

We said goodby to Jack, paid our bill and headed next door to the Lift&Pump.

We were greeted as always by Vince Luciano the gym owner-a 6 ft. black haired, blue eyed, very well put together 25 year old hottie with chiseled cheek bones and a very well connected family.

After our pleasantly distracting welcome, we stretched and hit the weights for our usual 45 minute stint.

The Lift & Pump is a no frills, basic, bare bones gym equipped with all the most up-to-date machines and weights. Also included are the low IQ muscle heads strutting their stuff in front of the mirrors, often distracting us from our reason for being there.

Chapter 4

At 5:00, we arrived at my house for dinner feeling limber and strong. We would need every bit of strength to drag information out of my Ombre.

We were both greeted with his usual bear hug. Very nice to come home to. Just have to remind myself not to get use to it.

He wasn't kidding. Dinner was fabulous. He made shrimp and chicken scampi with fresh broccoli, and extra garlic just the way I like it. It was to die for.

When we finished eating, mom and I cleared the table and did the dishes.

Mom always thinks better on a full belly. I however think better with wine, I opened a big bottle of Chardonnay and set it on the table. The three of us got down to business.

Ombre started by telling us........

"Last year while I was working for an un-named private investigation organization, I was contracted to follow a criminal prosecuting attorney for the State of New York to find out where she went, who she met with, and why."

"Her name is Andrea Livingston. I brought you a photo for identification purposes."

The photo shows a petite, professional looking attractive woman with shoulder length blonde hair, wispy bangs and blue-gray eyes. On the reverse side of the photo her height and weight is listed as 5'4" and 110 lbs. She is 49 years old.

"As fate would have it, she was someone from my past. I gathered the requested information and filed my report with the organization that hired me. Not knowing at the time how they were connected. As far as I was concerned, I did my job, did it well and I was done with it. End of story."

"Recently this same woman disappeared. Apparently having left work for a dinner meeting in her BMW and never came home that night. Her husband found the name Nick Salvatore in his wife's Rolodex and decided to contact him instead of the police because of a possible scandal or infidelity."

Nick earned a degree in journalism from SUNY Albany. He began his career as an intern and worked his way up to a top investigative reporter for the Albany paper he delivered as a teenager. Years of long days and nights have taken their toll on his personal life. Twice divorced, a chain smoker and beer drinker. He is 5'11" lanky with light brown stringy hair. His appearance wrinkled, disheveled and unkempt.

His words to live by, "News doesn't care what time it is."

"So, Nick gets involved and happens to have some knowledge of the criminal case she has been working on. He retraces her steps the night of her disappearance and found out that she made it to her dinner meeting with a not yet identified man. After the meeting, they left separately. She and her car were never seen again."

"Her husband is trying to make it look as though the unknown man is me. So, I think the husband is trying to set me up. Maybe he is some how involved with the people under indictment that his wife is prosecuting or she stumbled onto a ponzi scheme involving her husband."

"Either way the husband is feeding information regarding me to Nick."

I cannot believe that the man who gives no information to anyone has just told us an entire story start to finish leaving me with not one question.

As I look at mom she replies, "I got nothing, except a buzz. It's time for me to go now. Did we drink that whole bottle of Chardonnay? I need to go home now. I'll hook up with you tomorrow so we can discuss how we plan to approach our mission."

"Behave yourselves!"

Chapter 5

Tuesday morning I awoke at 5:30 am to the sound of my alarm, only to find that I am alone- no smell of coffee or breakfast- all alone. Ombre is back in the shadows. I couldn't help but wonder when he planned on appearing again.

So, doing my usual morning routine I head off to work.

My work day started with a little headache untouched by coffee and something tells me that my evening will end with an even bigger one.

That evening when I was driving down Central Avenue on my way to meet mom at the Pub I got to thinking about everything Ombre told us and how we would go about clearing his name.

I pull up in front of Fritzie's Pub, spotting mom's Tahoe parked out front. I stroll in seeing her talking to Jack at the bar. He smiles his usual glad to see ya smile as he poured my glass of wine. I hop on a stool next to mom as she smiles and says, "Missy I've been thinking."

"That's what I wanted to hear because I've been thinking to, and I got nothing."

"We should go to where she was last seen. So, how does dinner at Jack's Oyster House sound?"

"Works for me, they serve wine." Piling into mom's Tahoe, we head for Jack's.

Jack Rosenstein opened Jack's Oyster House in 1913 at the corner of Beaver and Green Streets. In 1937 Rosenstein moved the restaurant several blocks over to its' present location at the foot of State Street, a short walk down the hill from the New York State Capitol. Few restaurants have been under the ownership of a single family for that many decades. It is now run by Jack's grandson Brad Rosenstein preserving the restaurant's long standing traditions. They are now celebrating their 100th year anniversary. Hats off to them!

Mom starts to get excited. As we drive up, she spies what she claims to be the perfect parking place, making her whole day. She can just pull in without having to parallel park on the corner of State and Green Street.

We climb out of the truck and head down the sidewalk. After a couple of steps I realized I'm talking to myself. I look back to see mom starting down Green Street with a strange look on her face.

I yell over the traffic "Mom, what are you doing?"

"I'm not sure! I just got this really weird feeling that I was walking down Green Street. I can't explain it."

"Can we figure it out on a stool? I need a cocktail."

I looped my arm around hers and down State Street we went.

Entering Jack's we encountered the hostess, a young cutesy girl with long curly dark hair. She asked "Two for dinner?"

We asked if we could just sit at the bar?

"Sure" she said with a smile, "Right this way."

As we sit at the far most corner of the bar, by a small closet door, out of the way with a good view of the entrance and part of the diningroom, we try to get a feel of the atmosphere that Andrea would have experienced, the night she disappeared.

We order our wine and calamari. As we drink our wine, waiting for our snack, an elderly distinguished looking gentlemen passed by us opening the small closet door, peeked inside, then closed the door and walked back toward the entrance. After several more tiny peeks into the small closet-like room, mom and I couldn't help but wonder, just what was behind that door!

After finishing our calamari and cocktails, which were wonderful, by the way, we ventured outside to take a look around.

As we headed for the truck, I found I was talking to myself again. Mom was headed down
Green Street.
I yelled, "Mom where are you going? We did this already."
She kept walking as if in a daze right toward a young man wearing a white tank top, baggy jeans, a hat on sideways, and with tribal tattoos covering both arms. He was walking a brindle pit bull on a tow chain.
She walked right up to him and knelt down to pet his dog. The dog started wagging his tail and kissing mom's face. The hoodlum starts spewing profanity and yells to me "Get your crazy mother off my dog! I'm trying to teach him to be intimidating!"
With that, mom stood up perfectly straight, and I thought dear god hear it comes.
"How dare you! You little delinquent! Trying to poison the mind of a sweet little puppy. You ought to be ashamed of yourself. Did your mother raise you to do this sort of thing?"
He walked away whispering "crazy broad!"
That's when mom started telling me about a dream like vision of a man walking a dog up Green

Street. A well-dressed woman walking toward them, stopping to pet the dog, someone stepping out of a doorway behind her and covering her face with a cloth. As her body went limp, the two men picked her up and put her in her BMW. One pulling her keys from her purse and climbing behind the wheel. They drove off.

I asked, mom, "Where did that come from?"

With a pale shocked expression she said, "I have no idea! I saw the whole thing as though I was watching it happen."

"Since I was a little girl, I've had unexplained feelings and visions of things that either have happened or are about to happen.

As a child I remember my grandmother having similar experiences. My grandmother was part Native American. My mother was never really a believer in my grandmother's abilities, until I started having similar experiences. She now wishes she paid more attention. As far as we can tell this seems to skip a generation."

Chapter 6

The next evening after a long day's work and the gym, mom and I decide our next move is to go talk to Conrad.

I contact Conrad and ask to set up a meeting with him regarding his wife's disappearance. With that he replies, "What are you talking about!"

"Who told you Andrea is missing?"

"That information falls under our client confidentiality agreement."

"We have been contracted to look into her disappearance."

"I'm going to ask you one more time who hired you?"

"One more time I'm going to tell you, that's, confidential!"

"So you can help us or you can be our number one person of interest. It's your call."

"Alright, my house 6:00pm. I'll squeeze you into my busy schedule."

"Well isn't that nice of you, considering you really don't have a lot of options."

Upon arrival at Andrea and Conrad's estate we encountered a very large set of wrought iron gates that opened automatically as we drove up. Mom looked at me and said, "Wow! What exactly does he do for a living?"

I replied, "Apparently he's in the import export business."

Mom says. "Apparently we're in the wrong business."

Diving up the long, winding, perfectly paved driveway, we approach the most exquisite brick house with impeccably kept gardens filled with freshly bloomed spring flowers. Pulling in under the carport we parked and got out.

As we approach the front door, we are greeted by a very angry baffled looking Conrad with his expensive suit, Italian leather shoes and perfectly quaffed medium brown hair and empty brown eyes. At 6ft he is lanky, untoned, and unshaven with his 5 o'clock shadow.

From his point of view he is clever, intelligent, in control, and a shrewd businessman.

From our point of view he is arrogant and obnoxious and we only met the man two minutes ago.

Mom whispers "Now we know why no one has had a good thing to say about him".

I say, "I just looked at him and didn't like him."

He shuffles us into a lavish den to the right of the grand foyer.

The far most wall is lined with endless shelves of books. In front of them on a very plush oriental rug sits a large oak desk, with Andrea's computer, Rolodex, and a stack of legal file folders.

Facing the desk sit two large leather chairs. As Conrad rounds the desk, he motions for us to take a seat.

I sit down and take out my notebook, where I had jotted down a few basic questions. I started with:

"When was the last time you saw your wife?"

He replied, "On the morning of the day she disappeared."

"What day was that?"

"Friday morning."

"What was your conversation about that day?"

"I don't remember. Same as every other day. We don't talk much in the morning."

"How did she seem to you?"

"Was she nervous, apprehensive, secretive, distracted?"

"What difference does that make now, she's still gone."

"Did she give you any indication that something might be wrong?"

"No! Everything she does is confidential. She doesn't tell me anything about her work. Or her life for that matter."

"Do you have any idea what her schedule was for that day?"

"How would I know that? I just told you she doesn't tell me anything."

"Regarding your business dealings, are you involved in anything that could come back and bite her in the ass just because she's married to you?"

"My business dealings are none of your concern and have nothing to do with my wife's disappearance."

"Do you know who she met for dinner the night she disappeared?"

"She said she had a business dinner and she would be late, that was it."

"To your knowledge do you know of anyone who would want to harm Andrea"?

"No I don't. She's a criminal attorney. Im sure lots of people would like to get even with her."

"Do you remember what she was wearing."

"How the hell would I know? I don't keep track of her wardrobe."

While Jules was asking the questions, I was pacing back and forth scanning the room.

Conrad rudely dismissed us because he decided he was done with us.

With that I calmly walked up to him leaned down putting both my palms firmly on his desk. Smiling I looked him right in the face and said, "So tell me what were you two arguing about that morning?"

His mouth fell open and he went silent for a moment. Looking completely stumped he said, "How did you know that?"

"That doesn't matter if you want to help your wife. Answer the question."

He said, "You think you know everything figure it out!"

"Oh we will figure it out." And, if this leads back to you and whatever you're into, and we find out it has anything to do with her disappearance, we will personally blow your little empire right out of the water!"

As we head for the door I whisper "Bravo mom well done!"

She smiled and said "I got this".

Looking back at Conrad she said, "Thank you for meeting with us, and make no mistake, we will crack this case, and we will get her back with or without your help. Have a nice evening."

Walking toward the Tahoe mom says "I really don't like that man. He is a condescending little maggot!"

"What's to like?"

As we climb in the truck I ask,

"What exactly did you see back there?"

"I'm not really sure. It was a cloudy vision of a heated argument between the two of them. The whole conversation was negative energy. No specifics."

Chapter 7

Walking into Fritzie's Pub Thursday evening, we find our seats at the bar, settle in and Jack comes over with our wine in each hand and says, "I will only give you this if you promise to take her with you when you go." He nods toward the dance floor and there on the dance floor was my grandmother in all her glory, dressed in a spandex leopard print dress covered with fringes busting a move in her high heals.

As mom looks with a horrified expression, Nan (as I have always been instructed to call her because "grandma sounds to old") spots us and yells across the room......

"My Jules and Angel have arrived!"

Together we look back at Jack as he still holds our wine hostage he says, "Promise me."

Unfortunately we had to promise, and he relinquished our wine.

As we tried to tune out the antics on the dance floor, I ask mom "So, what's your take on Conrad?"

"He's definitely hiding something. His whole demeanor is off. For someone who's wife is missing he's very disconnected."

"So you think he had something to do with it?"

"I do."

"Why?"

"Because his mouth almost hit the desk when I asked him about the argument he had with his wife that day."

As Jack came over to chat, mom casually asked him "What do you know about Conrad Livingston?"

"Nothing good. I've heard some rumors, why?"

"We're looking into a case that involves him and his business.

"I have heard that his dealings are not exactly on the up and up."

"Well if you accidentally hear anything regarding him, could you let us know?"

"Sure" he said. "Just don't forget your promise to me."

Mom said, "I wouldn't do that to you, or anyone else."

We paid our bill, and my grandmother's, which was higher. She must have been there for a while.

I asked mom how she fits that much Chablis in that little 90 pound body. At 75 years old, 4'11" tall, red curly hair, brown eyes and an extremely explosive attitude mom says "She's had a hell of a lot of practice"!

Making our way to the dance floor to collect her, she made it quite clear she was not ready to call it a night. She said she had more dancing to do and she wasn't finished with her glass of wine yet.

With that mom and I each grabbed an arm and out the back door we went. As we head for the Tahoe, Nan tries to make an escape. Just then a car pulls in and parks right next to us. "Just great" mom says. "The whole dam parking lot and he has to park right next to us, until she see's who it is.

Vito climbs out from behind the wheel dressed in a waiters uniform.

"Would you like some assistance ladies?"

"That would be wonderful. She may be tinny but she's mighty."

Vito picks up nan and puts her in the back seat hits the lock and shuts the door.

With that we could hear her spewing curse words and pounding on the window.

"Thank you" mom said. "So what's with the uniform?" she asked with a grin as she turns her back to the obnoxious noise coming from the truck.

"You know me just looking into a few things in my spare time."

Vittorio Martino has been a judge for the past twenty years. At 58 years old, he thinks he has heard it all. But, every now and again he is unpleasantly surprised by a verdict. We often call him or just show up at his office if we need help or information on a case. He always acts like we are putting him out, but he always sees us and takes our calls.

He has been divorced from crazy Sheila for over twenty years now and they have two grown boys in their thirties.

Crazy Sheila. What can I say? Her name suits her. Every now and then she goes off the deep end or just off her medication. When she is on her meds, she is a bit strange to say the least. But, when she is off her meds, she is way off. Paranoid doesn't begin to cover it. She believes that mom is the devil and the root of all things evil in her world. She blames mom for all things bad with Vito. Occasionally she stalks us, which really makes things interesting when we are undercover on a case. Usually we can lose her. But, sometimes she has too much to drink and we end up taking her home after she makes a total fool of herself. Alcohol and psych meds do not mix.

He and mom went all through school together, so they know each other very well. A scenario my father hates.

He is one of a handful of our go-to-guys. From him, we get advice on all things legal and not.

Every now and again on a case of our own we run into him in the strangest places. Usually late at night and usually he is in disguise. Apparently, he does a bit of his own research on cases that don't end the way he thinks they should. It's a don't ask don't tell situation for all parties involved. That is what makes it a great working relationship. And, every now and then he enlists our help with information he can't get on his own for one reason or another. Sort of a friends in low places arrangement.

"What about you two? We haven't crossed paths in a while."

"We're working a new case about a missing attorney. She hasn't been reported missing yet. Her husband thinks she's having an affair. That's why he says he hasn't called the police."

"Did the husband hire you?"

"No."

"A friend asked us to look into it."

"What's the attorney's name?"

"Andrea Livingston."

Vito's jaw bounced off the ground.

Mom reading the shocked expression on his face asked him, "You know her?"

"Just from the court room."

"Do you know anything about her husband?"

"Only that he's no good."

"We learned that today."

"We met him to ask him some questions."

"He went out of his way not to help us. We got the impression he has no interest in finding her."

"If you hear anything about him or his so called import-export business, could you let us know?"

"Sure" he said, if you promise me you'll watch your backs. Like I said the guy is no good. I know he runs his business out of the Port, but that's about it. Keep me posted will ya?"

"Will do" mom said, as we parted ways.

Climbing into the Tahoe, we both turned to see my grandmother sound asleep in the back seat. I whisper to Mom "What was up with him? Did you catch that reaction?"

"How could I miss it?" "He lied when he said he new her only from court."

"How do you know?"

"Because I have known that man my whole life and something is really wrong for him to act like that. Which leads me to believe there is a lot more between them that he is not telling us. We need to know what is going on. Time to do a little digging."

We take my grandmother home to her bungalow. Once more each grabbing an arm up the steps to the front porch we go, passing the brightly colored angel flag flying in the light breeze. My grandmother has a fetish for angels. She has them everywhere, in every form, in every room, hence my mother's name.

Entering the front door into her livingroom it is dimly lit by her collection of Italian oil lamps and statues. Passing through the quiet house to the dining room, a loud voice starts chattering. Mom and I nearly drop Nan as we go for our guns with our free hands. "WHAT THE HELL?" Mom yells! Looking up hanging on the wall is a motion activated angel saying a prayer, while flapping her wings. My Nan bursts out laughing with the deepest belly laugh I have ever heard come out of her tiny body. She stops for just a second to squeeze out the words, "DON'T YOU JUST LOVE HER?" Then went right back to laughing.

By the time we got her to her bedroom, she had tears in her eyes from laughing. It was a chore to get her flannel angel jams on, but we triumphed in the end.

Tucking her into bed still laughing, we said good night. She said "Good night my sweethearts." We locked up and headed out.

Walking to the truck, I said to mom "That woman just took a year off my life with her weird shit."

"Welcome to my world."

Chapter 8

Friday, after a long day at work and the gym I arrive home to my usual greeting of hugs and kisses from my boys. After letting them out to pee, I got to thinking how complicated life can become in an instant. Just then my phone buzzed. Looking at the display, it said dad. My father hardly ever calls me, so I knew something was up.

When I answered, he said "Jules, I am taking mom to dinner tonight. I thought you might like to come."

"Sure. Where are we going?"

"I was thinking of the Olde Mystic Inn. We haven't been there in a while."

"Works for me.

What time?"

"Sixish?"

"I'll be ready."

I hung up and went to my room to look through

the closet. I found a nice white spring dress with tiny black flowers and spaghetti straps. How I have missed my summer wardrobe. On to the shoes. I broke out my favorite pair of six inch black strappy sandals. Looking at them, I thought, what a long winter.

I smiled and said to myself, it's official, summer has arrived!

Taking a shower and getting dressed, I felt great in my summer ensemble.

I slapped some makeup on my face and headed for the stairs.

When I got to the bottom, I heard a commotion.

My boys came flying down the hall all excited.

Looking up, my Ombre was at the other end grinning.

"What are you doin here?" I asked.

"Hopefully, going anywhere with you he replied. You look fabulous. Do we have a date?"

"No. I am going to dinner with my parents."

"Well then, he said with a relieved expression, dad would love it if I came along."

"Why? Do I look like I need a date?"

"Oh no honey. You look like you need a team of body guards."

I gave him a faint smile and said, "I don't think dad would mind if you crashed."

When mom and dad pulled in my driveway to pick me up, he got the what the hell are you doing here look from mom and the yes look from dad.

Walking down the driveway to mom's Tahoe and climbing in, I was thinking, even now at 35 years old, I still don't want to have to explain this to mom.

"This is different," she said.

I thought, here it comes.

"You decide to do your sneakappear thing tonight? Bless us with your presence. Well, aren't we lucky?"

"Come on mom. Don't be like that. I missed you."

"Yeah, yeah, yeah."

"I said can we please just have a nice peaceful dinner?"

He whispered in my ear, "Dressed like that, you can have whatever you want."

"I heard that", mom said as we pulled out of the driveway.

By dusk, we were finally approaching the Inn. My father is known for taking the longest possible route to anywhere. He will drive ten miles out of his way for what he claims to be better roads for a better ride.

Pulling into the lot the old relic of a building always looks inviting with it's two stories and white square pillars. The upstairs has a few rentable rooms that lead out to a cozy front porch. There is one attic window with a rocking chair in it. Some say it moves by itself at certain times. The building has a long history of having spirts of both kinds. The basement, years and years ago, was rumored to have been used as a jail with stone rooms used as solitary confinement. The present day main floor is one of the best restaurants in the area. Our personal favorite.

We usually go for special occasions or just to kick off summer.

Climbing out of the Tahoe, dad and Ombre were in an in-depth military conversation about ten steps in front of us.

Mom and I in heals, trailed behind.

As we headed up the sidewalk, mom started to slow and said I always get the strangest vibrations just walking near this place. It feels as though someone or something is trying to communicate with me.

To our surprise, as the words left her lips, the entire front of the building lit up. White lights from the pillars and all the trees glowed as bright as day. It was beautiful.

We all stopped and looked at each other and then everyone looked at mom.

Her chest tightened as she said, "What? Don't look so surprised. It's not like it's new".

Entering the front door, the two heavyset blonde girls with chemically lightened hair, daughters of the owner, Buffy and Hildy rushed passed us to look out the window. One saying to the other,

"Would you look at that. Those lights have been broken for over a month."

Coming back to greet us, one said "Good evening. Four for dinner?"

Dad answered, "Yes please."

The other looked at mom and me and said "We are having a spring drawing. If you put your business card in the vase, you could win dinner and prizes" and she pointed to the big clear vase on the front desk half full of business cards.

I said, "Why not? You can't win if you don't play".

I pulled a Soul Sisters card from my purse and tossed it in the vase.

I said to mom, "Oh darn".

"What"? she replied.

"I should have had you kiss it first."

"Kiss this" she said as she smiled and headed toward the table, where dad and Ombre were already sitting, still in the same conversation.

Crossing the floor alongside mom we passed over a large wrought iron heat vent in the floor. Just then a quick, cold, burst of air came shooting out of it sending my dress clear up into my armpits. Mom was over just far enough that hers barely moved.

Looking over at me she said, "Really? A thong? You know I hate it when you wear those things."

Dad and Ombre were both staring at us with smirks on their faces.

I shuttered at the shock. Turning to mom, I said, "Do you think anyone saw?"

Looking around at the half full restaurant, everyone was staring at us.

Mom, said "Oh, I don't know. What do you think fancy pants?"

I looked at her and said, "Everyone hates a smart mouth. Someone told me that more than once."

Finally arriving at our table, Barnibus wonders over grinning. The spirts always get a little playful when the two of you come in he said.

"It's not me. It's her" I said pointing to mom.

"I just get dressed up and come along to be embare-ass-ed by a dam spirit. Everyone has a good laugh at my expense."

Barnibus Nistor, the owner of the inn migrated from Romania some thirty years ago with his wife Ava and two daughters. He has a mysterious almost dark persona because of his black wiry hair and ebony ivory eyes that seem to have no center contrasted by his snow white glistening skin.

Leaving us with menus to look over, he said, "Hopefully the entities that be will now let you relax and enjoy your dinner."

He then sent us over a round of drinks.

I suspect feeling a little bad about my embare–ass–ment.

Cocktails always make everything better. Especially when they're free.

After, ordering, eating, and wrapping what little was left, we were all stuffed. The food was wonderful.

Settling up our bill, it was time to go.

I was quite nervous about my exit. So I bunched my dress in one hand and held it tight until we got outside. I made it with no further incidents.

Just when we pulled from the lot all the lights went out again.

Part way home everyone was chatting about my horror when mom said to Ombre "Where should we drop you?"

Reading between the lines, not wanting to piss her off, he smirked and said "Anywhere downtown is fine."

"Are you sure"? Dad asked.

"He's sure" said mom.

As he climbed out of the truck smiling back at us, he said "Thank you for the dinner and peep show."

Chapter 9

Early Saturday afternoon, finishing work, I called mom to ask her what she thinks about taking a ride down to the Port to have a look around Conrad's empire.

"If there is a chance we can bring it down, I would love to. I did promise him you know."

"Yes you sure did."

"Meet me at the cloud. We can take the Tahoe. You can drive because I have a new case file to run by you."

"I will be there in ten minutes."

Getting behind the wheel waiting for mom, she comes down the steps of the brownstone with her giant bag of goodies. The bag is bustin at the seams with one liter bottles of water, protein bars, case files, binoculars and areal maps of the port.

"Could you fit anymore shit in that five pound sack?"

"Just thought you might like a snack. Nobody likes a smart mouth."

As we arrive, there is not much going on. Not wanting to get out of the truck to look, on account of the crime rate, we pull out our binoculars and do a quick scan to no avail.

We decide to head up Green Street toward the bridges and take a left on Madison Avenue, then a right on South Pearl Street past the Mac Donald's.

As we go by the Convention Center and the old National Savings Bank mom says "I'm getting a really weird feeling, pull over for a minute."

Crossing State Street on to North Pearl Street and passing the Palace Theater, I look for a place to pull over. When I find one, I ask "What do you see?"

Mom replies, "I see weird things but, I know it has something to do with Andrea."

Grabbing for my trusty pad and pen I start writing, as she lists off "I see 787, the river, old insulation, lots of stairs, a multi floor concrete building."

"I GOT THIS, I KNOW WHERE SHE IS!!!!!"

"Drive" she says.

I put my foot to the floor. "Ok where am I going?"

"Take a right on Wilson Street and head toward Central Warehouse."

Old Central Warehouse was built in 1927. Originally it was a cold - dry storage building before retailers maintained facilities on their own. The 400,000-square foot building held most of the Capital District's frozen food , but has been vacant since the 1980's. What used to be a busy freezer storage business, is now an abandoned eyesore with not much around it.

"Please tell me she hasn't been locked up in that god awful place all this time."

"I sure as hell hope not, but from what I just saw, that's the most likely place it jives with my vision."

As we pull up out in front on the lower level, mom says "How do we get in there?"

The entire lower level is surrounded in high chain link fence.

We climb out of the Tahoe and start to look around. In sync, as always, we both look up. On the second floor there is an indoor train station. I said to mom "How do we get up there?"

We both follow along the train trestle over Erie Street with our eyes. "What do you think?" I asked? "Well you know I'm not fond of heights."

Across the street there is a set of open back metal, mesh stairs going up to the trestle. "Lets give it a shot she says, but I don't like looking through the stairs, it makes me dizzy."

Crossing the street, we start up the stairs at a pretty good clip. As we get to the top mom starts to slow down, and says "I hate these."

"I know, just don't look down."

"I'm trying not to."

We slowly cross over the trestle. The old rotting, wooden boards are not in good shape. With the pieces missing we can see the cars passing below us.

"I turned to see mom standing still, looking down, saying "I DON'T LIKE THIS!" as the headlights rush by under her feet.

When she finally gets to the other side, a man appears out of nowhere and starts yelling at us. A little, short, portly fellow with a bald head yelling "YOU CANT BE UP HERE". His reflector vest logo indicates he works for the train company.

Mom and I run back in the other direction, while we are carefully trying to cross the trestle at a high rate of speed, the sky opens up and it starts to pour. Getting to the stairs with mom right on my heels, she yells "HOLLY CRAP. THESE GOT SLIPPERY!" The next thing I feel is mom on my back, and the two of us rolling down the last couple stairs, crashing into the muddy pit at the bottom. The portly mean man was standing at the top of the stairs still yelling. In sync, as always we both look up and yell "SHUT THE HELL UP!" Fumbling in the slippery mud, we rush to right ourselves, get to our feet and run like hell covered in mud, across the street, in the truck and took off. After a few long moments of silence, I said to her, "You are so going to help me clean out this truck."

"I will. I'm sorry. I slipped."

Mom says "We'll have to come back tonight but, we need another way in."

"Good cause I am not going through that again with you. It was too painful."

"I can't help it." "You know I don't like heights."

"Suck it up sister. That's what you always tell me."

"I need to take my own advise."

Around back we spy a large gate with a big pad lock on it. As we slow up to examine it, mom looks at me and says "Bolt cutters".

In the rear view mirror I looked just in time to see an Albany Cop fly by. I grabbed a quick right hit the back roads and got out of there. Getting up to North Pearl Street, passing two more cops, looking down, there were four APD cruisers surrounding the warehouse.

I said to mom, "That bastard called the cops on us."

"Maybe he thinks we're terrorists, trying to blow the place up."

"The sissy girl kind that are afraid of a trestle."

"Hey, terrorists come in all shapes and sizes."

"We would be doing them a favor."

"These terrorist need a cocktail".

"We can't go anywhere looking like this."

"Let's go back to my cloud and get cleaned up. I just bought a case of wine."

"That's the best idea I have heard all day. Do you think you can do it without falling on your ass?"

"Don't be a smart mouth. It is very unbecoming."

Back at the cloud, thankfully the rain was letting up. Climbing out I glanced at the front seat in horror. Mom says "Don't waste a worry. We can fix it". I said "Yes we can".

Making our way up the not so slippery steps to the cloud, we both look up to see my father leaning in the doorway with a large grin on his face. He says "I don't even want to know."

Walking past dad, giving him a dirty look, without much expression, with that much mud it is easy to do, we head for the kitchen. He follows the muddy trail behind us.

"Open the wine, mom says to dad. We need to get cleaned up."

"You take the guest bathroom and I'll take our bathroom."

"Alright. I'll meet you back here."

Dad says, "I'll open the wine, but wouldn't it be easier to not get dirty in the first place?"

"Everybody's a smart mouth today" mom says as she stomps up the stairs.

Chapter 10

By the time mom came down stairs all clean and fresh, the late afternoon sun was starting to peek through the clouds. I had already printed up a floor plan of Central Warehouse off mom's computer and was sitting on the back deck with dad looking it over with my much needed wine.

Snagging the glass of wine dad had left her on the kitchen island, she came through the sliding glass doors to join us on the deck. Stepping out she stopped, looked up and said "Finally some sun. What a difference from and hour ago." As she sat down, she said "Oh good. You found us some direction. I hate flying blind."

The three of us planned our best way in and where to go once inside. We then made our list of what to bring with us.

Bolt cutters, 9 millimeters, mace, stun gun, tie

ties, bottled water, flashlights, protein bars, an extra jumpsuit, some gloves and a first aid kit, just in case.

"We need to bring my truck." "After today they know yours."

Just then, something caught my eye below us. I said to mom "Who is that? And why haven't you introduced us?"

"Oh. That's our new tenant, Dameon. He just moved in yesterday."

"You let someone named Dameon move into Angel's cloud"?

"What can I say? I like him".

"And I'm liking the new view from your deck".

Dameon looks up smiles and waves.

As it starts to get dark, we put on our black jump suits, pack up our back packs, and load up my truck. "I drive a 2001, dark cherry red Dodge Ram extended cab pickup with tinted windows."

Later that night heading out on our mission, pulling in about two blocks away from the warehouse on De Witt St., we get out and stalk our way between two old warehouses and the train tracks careful to stay hidden in the shadows. Working our way toward the warehouse, we come to the dead end of Colonie Street waiting and watching for a moment to make sure no one else is around.

Over the Jersey barrier and heading for the

gate, I say to mom "Now is a good time to get those bolt cutters out."

"I'm already on it".

She pops the lock. Moving the gate, we slide inside. As we do, I reset the gate and the lock so as not to be detected.

We head for the building to a small opening once covered by plywood placed after the fire, now torn off by homeless people who occupy the place.

Once inside the smells hits us - damp, burnt, urine soaked, musty, stinky place.

Something tells us if she is in here she's more than ready to be found.

Flashlights in hand, wondering forward, we round a corner to the left and almost land on a large covered item. Mom lifts it and says, "I knew it, we found her BMW. Now lets go find her. I know she's in here somewhere."

According to the floor plan, we come to the first set of stairs, scan the first floor - some open spaces, some little rooms, debris all over the floor, glass, old furniture.

We continue up to the third floor more debris all over. It's like every room, every floor has it's own theme. Mom says "Look at this." There was one whole room where the entire floor was covered with nuts and bolts.

We come upon the fifth floor and piles of old hub caps.

"Who carries these up five flights of stairs and for what?"

"I'm guessing the same people who carry up all the cans of spray paint to design all this graffiti."

"Someone has way to much time on their hands. I'm just sayin. Time not well spent."

Reaching the seventh floor we start hearing noises. I said to mom "I don't think we're alone any more."

We heard a loud thump ahead of us.

"I whisper that was not a pigeon."

As always, in perfect sync, we both put one hand on our guns. Rounding the next corner a homeless man in a dirty trench coat jumps out in our path yelling "Give me your money"!

We both draw guns and point them at his head.

He stood there wide eyed for a moment then turned tail and ran yelling "Sorry to have bothered you, carry on."

"Dam it" I said to mom "If you didn't scare the hell out of him, we could have used him for information."

"Me, why did I scare him? You did the same thing I did."

"Yeah, but you gave him the look."

"He could not have seen my look with two flashlights and two guns in his face."

"I'm just saying. Let's be a little nicer to the next one. Maybe we can pump them for some much needed information."

"Couldn't hurt. Were running out of floors."

As we reach the tenth floor we're running out of hope, and getting tired. Mom says "I'm gonna see peeling paint in my sleep tonight."

We scan along opening doors.

This floor has a lot of small rooms. We come upon a freezer room on our left with a closed door and a pad lock on it.

Mom says "This is it. She's in there".

She pulls the bolt cutters off her belt once more and snips the lock.

I push the door open and there curled up in a tiny ball in the corner of the small, cold room shivering is Andrea.

Mom says "Andrea?"

"We have been looking all over for you!"

"Who are you she asks?"

I said "A friend of yours asked us to find you, and keep safe. We are private investigators. My name is Jules and this Angel. We have to move."

"I'm a nurse" mom says. "Are you hurt?"

"No, I'm just starving."

"Can you walk?" mom asks as she helps her to her feet.

Andrea says "I can run if it means getting out of here."

As mom turns around, I reach into her back pack, pull out a black jumpsuit, a bottle of water, and a protein bar. We help her into the suit, hand her the bottle of water and the snack and move as fast as possible toward the stairs.

Ten flights down went a lot faster than ten flights up. We reach the bottom, go out the way we came in, stop frequently to listen and look to make sure were alone, cross to the gate, sneak through the gate, once more setting the bolt, cross Colonie St., help Andrea over the Jersey barrier and behind the buildings, get back to the truck and take off.

Chapter 11

As soon as we get rolling, Andrea says "Can you please hit up the first drive-thru we come to. I can't tell you how long I've been in there but I do know it's been a while since I've had real food."

"No problem" mom says. "We are just so glad we found you. You can have what ever you want."

Pulling up to MacDonald's she orders a big mac, large fries and a large ice tea.

By the time we get back to my house, all the food is gone.

"I feel so much better" she says climbing out of my truck with her empty food wrappers.

"We have something else that's gonna make you feel better. How about a nice hot shower, some clean jammies, and a nice warm bed?"

"That sounds like heaven to me!" We show her around my tiny house, introduce her to my boys and her room, then she hits the shower.

So mom says, "Tell me what our next move is."

"Well, first we call Ombre and tell him we have her. Then, when she comes out of the shower, we need to ask her some questions and see what she knows."

"Lets make a list."

1. Who was she with at Jack's on Friday?

2. Did she leave alone?

3. What happened next? Where were you parked? Where did you go?

4. What is your next memory?

5. What case were you working on?

6. Why did no one from your office report you missing?

Just then, she came out of the shower.

"We have a few questions for you."

"Can we talk in the morning? I'm exhausted. I need to sleep in a warm, dry, safe place."

"No problem." "Tomorrow is another day."

"Are you sure this is a safe place?"

I told her "As long as whoever it is that took you thinks you are still locked in the warehouse, you are safe. No one would look for you here anyway. That's why you need to stay hidden".

"I am here to tell you, no one will get anywhere near this house without my boys knowing about it."

"If by some slim chance they did, I sleep with a 9 millimeter on my bedside table. Bottom line, don't waste a worry. The boys only allow my parents and my best friend to just walk in. You can sleep tight. You are probably safer here than you ever were in your own house."

Andrea smiles and says "Thank you. You don't know what this means to me", as she heads down the hall to the spare room. "See you in the morning."

I call Ombre.

"We found her. She is here and she is safe."

"I will be right there."

Mom says, "It has been too long a day. I'm tired, hungry and dirty and I need to go home. I'll be back first thing in the morning. I want to be here for the questioning."

"Alright, I will see you then."

As I walked mom out, closed the door, turned around, I bounced off Ombre in my living room.

"Why the hell do you have to sneakappear?"

He smiles and says, "You've been busy."

"Yes we have."

"Where is she?"

"Sound asleep in the spare room."

"Where did you find her?'

"She was in cold storage, on the tenth floor in Central Warehouse."

"How the hell did you know that?"

"Mom had a vision."

"You have got to be kidding!"

"I'll explain later. I need a shower. I have no

idea what I have been exposed to tonight. Had I had a clue, I would have brought my hazmat suit."

He just grinned.

As I headed for the bathroom, he followed.

Chapter 12

Early the next morning Andrea opens her eyes to yet another unfamiliar place. Slowly remembering what has happened and where she is.

Heading for the bathroom, she stumbles out into the hallway and bounces off of Ombre wearing only his boxer shorts.

"What the hell are you doing here?"

He just smiles and says, "Funny meeting you here."

"You did this."

"You had them find me."

I hear the commotion and head for the hall.

As I get there, mom comes in the front door.

"What the hell is going on? And, why am I the only one dressed?"

With all the commotion and company the boys got all excited, started flailing and ran for the back door like two bulls in a china shop, wanting to be let out to pee.

We all start laughing, as we scatter between the bedroom, bathroom and kitchen.

Ombre yells, "I am going to build something for breakfast."

Mom yells back "Build a lot of it. We can't seem to fill her up.

And, put some pants on."

"You got it mom."

A short time later - all dressed, we converge on the kitchen to the aroma of coffee, toast, and an enormous pan of eggs.

After breakfast, we put on another pot of coffee and get down business.

We start with the list of questions that mom and I made while Andrea was in the shower.

The first one being:

"Who did you meet at Jack's on Friday?"

"I don't see where that is relevant."

"It has nothing to do with whoever took me."

"I know that for a fact."

"Okay, we'll get back to that."

"Did you leave alone?"

"Yes."

"What happened next?"

"Where did you park?"

"Where did you go?"

"I parked on Green Street and walked toward my car. I saw a man walking a dog. When I stopped to pet the dog, someone grabbed me from behind and put something over my nose and mouth. That was the last thing I remember."

Mom sits up and says "I knew it. That's exactly what I saw".

"What was your next memory?"

"Waking up in the warehouse scared to death."

"Why did none of your co-workers call to report you missing?"

"I was going to New York City for a few days to follow up on a case I have been working on."

"Can you tell us a little bit about the case? Any information you give us will be confidential and will help us figure out what is going on."

"I know you are all trying to help me but, I really can't divulge any information about the case."

"Okay. Is there anyway Conrad can be involved in your case or your disappearance?"

Slowly as the wheels start to turn, she replies "I don't think so. I hadn't thought of that."

Ombre says, "Are you sure?"

"No, no I am not."

"We need to know who the mystery man was you had dinner with that night because your husband is trying to make it look as though it was me. He was trying to set me up for your disappearance."

"How do you know that?"

"We all have our secrets. You need to stay here, out of sight, where it is safe, until we figure this out."

"I can live with that."

"You can't contact anyone. No one can know you are not still in that warehouse."

Mom says, "The three of us have to work out a surveillance of the warehouse around our schedules."

I say, "Today is my day off, so I will do today."

"Mom is off on Monday which leaves nights and everyone knows Ombre works better in the moonlight."

"This weekend we will swap up."

Just then mom's cell phone rings. She answers it and says "We will be right down."

Mom says "Jules we have a lead."

"We will be back in an hour."

As we exit, I say "What's going on mom?"

"Jack has information for us. We need to get to Fritzie's."

Chapter 13

Walking in the door, the bar is empty. Jack is setting up for his usual busy day. He smiles and says "Come sit."

He begins by telling us "Some of the longshoreman were in talking about something going on at Central Warehouse this week."

"It appears to be Wednesday night and it doesn't look good. But, I didn't get too much detail other than one of the big bosses is coming in from Jersey to meet with Conrad at the Port."

Chapter 14

The atmosphere is charged.

It is never a good sign when the bosses come up. Pasquale (Patsy) Cantone wants a meeting with Conrad to discuss his wife. She has too much information on Conrad's business and Patsy's organization and needs to be dealt with.

Patsy, a life long product of his environment, knows how to get what he wants. At 40 years old, 160 lbs, he has a dark dangerous, cold stare with almost black eyes, and a soulless ora. He has an olive complexion and the most exquisite set of dimples you would ever want to see. He knows just when they can be useful and how to use them to the fullest extent of his advantage, making every women in his path have to step back and gain some perspective. Men, on the other hand, are usually so intimidated, they can't get away from him fast enough. The pack mentality kicks in and they are reduced to the bottom of the pecking order within the first minute in his presence.

At the meeting, Patsy tells Conrad "Wednesday night two of my men will be disposing of her. We were hoping it wouldn't come to this but, we now have no choice. Your wife is too good at what she does. If only she worked for us."

"There is no chance of that ever happening. So just do what needs to be done."

"I will be in touch when it is time for you to do your part, when the dates of the incoming shipment are confirmed."

Chapter 15

Back at my house Andrea and Ombre are waiting to hear what we have learned.

"Our sources told us that Wednesday night there is something big going down at Central Warehouse."

"It sounds as though they have decided what they are going to do with you and they are coming for you on Wednesday night."

"So, we won't need our surveillance plan. Wednesday night we will ALL get to see who THEY are."

Ombre asks Andrea - "You really have no idea who these people are?"

"I really don't have a clue who would do this to me."

"Is there any possibility this has anything to do with your case?"

"I suppose it could, but I can't give you any specific information."

Mom says "LOOK, after today we know for a

fact that your husband and Patsy Cantone are behind your disappearance. So before this comes to bite all of us in the ass for helping you, you need to tell us what you know. This is the mob we are dealing with."

With a shocked, sad expression she says "We have been having some problems lately, but I never in my wildest dreams would have thought he could do this to me."

Ombre says, "With all of our history together, do you trust me?"

She looks at him with a sad smile and says - "With my life."

With that he moves across the room. Sitting next to her, he put one of his massive arms around her shoulder. As she leans in and puts her head on his chest, her tears start to flow.

As I watch this unravel, I see the connection they still share and I am overwhelmed with a pang of jealousy I shouldn't feel.

He quietly whispers to her, "You have to tell us what we need to know. I have put two very important people in my life in danger to help you. Now, you need to help me fix it."

With a deep sigh she says, "My case revolves around Cantone. We are trying to indict him on a number of charges. That is why I was going to NYC to meet with the DA to combine the information we have gathered and come up with a list of charges for the indictment. I knew he was working with someone at the Port, but I had no idea it was Conrad."

"That doesn't help us much."

"We all need to sleep on it."

When mom leaves, Ombre walks her to her truck and does not return. He is back in the shadows again.

After they left Andrea and I decide to have a nightcap. We opened a bottle of red and hit the livingroom.

As we got to talking, Andrea started telling me about the area's top heavy hitters and how they came to be.

She said, "Every cop, PI and bounty hunter's dream is to find the true identity of the man or woman known only as Sorius."

"Rumor has it Sorius and Cantone have been extreme rivals for years. Apparently, some years ago they got together and called a truce. Only the two of them know the rules of the agreement. Cantone is the only one to have ever laid eyes on Sorius in the flesh. And, as usual, he is not talking."

"What they do for a living usually only ends one way. So, for them both to still be breathing now, it is my personal belief that they have surrounded themselves with people in very high places. When I stop and think about it I am extremely jealous. They have no rules. If Soul Sisters had those kinds of resources, think of the possibilities. The mysteries you could solve. The two of you could rule the world."

"I love that thought and we just might build our own circle". Smiling back at her I said "I think I'll dream on it right now."

We locked up the house and went to bed.

Chapter 16

Monday morning I head out for work. Mom comes over to hang out with Andrea. Ombre is still in the shadows.

Mid afternoon mom calls me and says "What we all need is a pre- sting party. What do you think?"

"Party? I like it."

"Stop by the store on your way home and pick up a few things. Surprise me. I talked to dad and told him to be here at five."

"Okay." "I will call Ombre and let him know."

The surprise is beef tenderloin, shrimp and lots of cocktails.

As we fire up the grill, dad and Ombre appear.

Dad with his usual chips and dip in hand (he always brings chips and dip), and Ombre brings himself.

So we hand him the very large piece of meat, and the men head for the back yard.

The women head for the kitchen to open the wine. When it starts to flow, it never stops.

We all had a wonderful dinner. Dad takes home a very happy mom. Andrea passes out with a full belly and a much needed buzz. Ombre puts her to bed.

When he walked out of her room, closing the door behind him, I wanted to ask him just how they came to be acquainted. But, I refrained because it just didn't matter. He may very well be gone by morning. He isn't mine and we don't have a claim on each other.

Taking one look at the expression on my face, he asked, "What's wrong"?

"It just doesn't matter tonight. Are you staying or going?"

"Is that an invitation?"

I just smiled and walked toward my bedroom.

As he followed, I heard him murmur, "I'll take that as a yes."

After a very long week, and lots of cocktails, it felt great to cozy up next to a warm buff body. In his powerful arms, just for tonight, I could forget about the rest of the world.

As I kiss him and rake my nails down his back, I said, "Something tells me we are not going to get much sleep tonight."

"I hope not" and flips me onto my bed.

Fully aroused and wide awake, my heart started to pound. Kissing my neck. The mere scent of him swamps me with desire as I run my hands down his hot damp skin.

My breath caught in my chest. He looked right at me and produced the smirk. Goose bumps ran down every inch of my body.

I could feel his heated breath on my neck as he whispered "I've missed you."

No one else has ever had this kind of effect on me. He just touches me and my entire body melts down.

I've missed him to. I've missed this but I won't say it out loud.

Chapter 17

All day Wednesday, we are nervously calm, anticipating what is to come.

6:00 pm the four of us meet at my house, planning to be at the warehouse by 7:00 to give us time to find an inconspicuous place to park the truck where we will have a good view of the back gate and not be noticed.

With us we will bring guns, flashlights, tie ties, bolt cutters, binoculars and mom's high tech first aid kit. She never leaves home without it.

Ombre looks at her and says, "I thought you were bringing a first aid kit?"

"I did", holding it up.

"That's not a kit, that's luggage."

She smiles and says "You may need me one day and I will be prepared".

"For a natural disaster maybe". We pack up my

Dodge, head down town, stopping at a drive thru along the way for Andrea's snacks. Not knowing when this is going down, we'll probably be in the truck for a while.

Eleven minutes to 7:00 we do a drive by the back gate. All is quiet as we pass.

Backing the truck into the shadows at an old abandoned business on DeWitt St. with a clear view of the gate, we settle in.

Ombra says, "This is where we go our separate ways".

As he climbs out of the truck quietly shutting the door, he disappears into the shadows.

Mom says, "I love the way he looks in his camo. Reminds me of how handsome your dad used to look in his Navy Blues."

8:02 a black Cadillac Escalade with tinted windows and Jersey plates slowly drives by the back gate of the warehouse.

Mom says, "We have activity."

We all slide down in our seats, raising our binoculars, as it goes by us, turns around, heads back toward the gate and parks.

Two men, all in black, climb out look around, and head for the gate.

They stop dead and look at each other when they realize the bolt has been cut. Still looking around they head for a door at the back of the building, and disappear inside.

All of a sudden from the back seat Andrea yells! "That's the guy. That's the guy with the dog from Green St!" She drops her binoculars in shock.

Mom says "YES! Yes it is. I saw him too! Now were getting somewhere.".

Andrea say, "Okay, when this is all over you and I are going to need to get together so you can explain this whole vision thing to me".

"Done" mom says.

"It's going to be a while. They've got 10 flights to climb" Jules says.

At 8:30 they reach the 10th floor. Heading down the hallway they see the once bolted-shut door wide open. They look at each other and say, "What the hell? Who could have known she was here?"

Panicked! Not wanting to have to tell Patsy, they call Conrad.

"She was hidden in Central Warehouse. We just came here to collect her and she's gone. Patsy is not going to like this. We have to find her NOW. Get yourself down here. We need to search this dump from top to bottom."

"I'm on my way."

Hanging up he calls Nick.

"Nick, I need help. You're the only other person who knows Andrea is missing. I just found out that she's been held at Central Warehouse. We need to go and see if we can find her."

"I'll meet you there in five minutes."

"Ok. I'll wait for you at the back gate."

Nick hangs up and immediately calls Ombre and tells him "Conrad just called me to say Andrea is somewhere in Central Warehouse and he needs help finding her. I'm to meet him at the back gate in five minutes."

Ombre answers, "I'm already there."

As the line goes dead, Nick whispers to himself, "What do you mean you're already there?"

Back at the truck another car pulls up to the gate.

Andrea says "That's Conrad's car."

A few seconds later another car pulls up, and Nick gets out.

Andrea says, "That's Nick. You've got to be kidding me. This just keeps getting better and better all the time. Nick and I have been friends all of our lives. How can he be mixed up in this?"

Conrad and Nick run into the building. All is quiet for a while. The three of us sit anxiously waiting, focused on the back door with our binoculars.

Andrea says, "Who the hell else in my world could possibly show up?"

"I don't know you've got to be running out of people by now!"

We sit in silence for a while watching.

Just then the back door flies open and the first mob guy comes running out with Conrad on his heals and Nick right behind them.

Mom yells "Where is the other mob guy?"

Right then Ombre appears in the shadow of the doorway.

"That answers that question."

As Ombre goes for the second mob guy, Nick takes down Conrad.

A speechless Andrea says "What the hell just happened?"

All at once everything lights up, and what we think is the entire Albany Police Department descends from all directions.

They take into custody, the two mob guys and Conrad.

As the three of us run toward Nick and Ombre at the scene, A car screeches to a halt and Vito steps out.

When they slap the cuffs on Conrad, he glares at Nick with disdain and says "I trusted you and you betrayed me."

Nick walks right at him, gets within inches of his face and says,

"Not nearly as much as you betrayed your wife."

As Nick stomps away, Conrad watches him walk toward his future ex-wife wrapped in Vito's arms.

Melting down, he screams Andrea's name over and over as the two officers wrestle him into the police car and drive off.

A speechless Andrea looks up at a smiling Vito and says "Your going to have to explain this to me. I am so confused right now."

As we all meet together, Andrea says, "Who the hell wants to go first?"

Mom smiles at Vito and says, "You followed us didn't you?"

"With all my favorite women wrapped up in this, I had to make sure everyone was safe."

He smiles, wraps his arms around Andrea and says "How about I take you home?"

After Vito and Andrea leave, Nick tells us how happy he is that she is alright and Conrad is going where he belongs.

"I never did like that guy."

Mom says "I need to get home." "It has been a long day." I need a drink and some sleep."

"Me too." "I'll drop you home." "Just let me grab Ombre and we are out of here."

Looking around I realize Ombre is already gone. Go figure.

"Does that shock you?"

I shot her a look.

"I'm just saying. That's what he does."

Chapter 18

The following afternoon, we all meet at Fritzie's for our victory celebration.

Jack greets us at the door, hugging mom and me he whispers, I'm glad everything turned out so well! Mom says, "It may not have without you"! He squeezes us both and goes back behind the bar.

We leave dad chatting with Jack and go to greet Andrea and Vito, as Nick comes in behind them.

Before we sit down to dinner dad asks me if Ombre is coming?

"I was hoping, but you just never know with him."

Andrea asks mom and me, "Can I speak to the two of you for a minute?"

We wander off to a quiet corner of the bar.

Getting our drinks she says, "For the two of you to do what you did for me, having not even known me, there are no words to express my gratitude. I could have died there or they could have killed me. No one would have ever known what happened to me!"

Just then the door opened and Ombre saunters in smiling at me. Coming over to join us he said, "My three favorite girls all together and still alive!"

We all start to laugh.

Andrea says "I'm glad you came. I was just thanking Angel and Jules and I need to thank you to."

She looks at mom and me and says, "If there is ever anything the two of you need, always remember I'm just a phone call away."

Mom and I smile at each other and whisper, "Secret Circle."

"I second that Vito says as he strolls up behind her and puts an arm around her. You all made me realize how much she means to me, and I hope she feels the same way."

Smiling up at him she says, "Of course I do my mystery dinner date." As we all look at each other and burst out laughing, dad yells! "LETS EAT!"

Walking toward the table Vito asks mom "Have you seen Sheila?"

Mom says "No not in a while."

Vito says "That's odd neither have my sons."

After finishing a wonderful dinner in great company, everyone was chatting and having a good time. I said to mom, "I am going to the ladies room. Do you want to come with?"

"Sure" she said as she stood and grabbed her bag. "I need to move I ate too much."

On the way back to the table we stopped at a now packed bar for our last glass of wine with Jack.

As he approached us with a very unusual look in his eyes, he said, "I just heard a rumor that concerns the two of you."

"Really, what did you hear?"

"Cantone is not at all happy about losing two of his best men to the legal system. He is out to get revenge on the people responsible."

Mom and I look at each other in perfect time and say, "This should be interesting."

Later that night, I curled up in my bed with a new crime novel and my boys. After all the day's activity, it didn't take long for me to start fading. Taking off my glasses and turning off the light, I rolled over and went unconscious.

Midnight on the dot, my boys went nuts - heavy into security breach mode. They both dove off the bed and ran for the stairs. I was right behind them, on me feet, 9 millimeter in hand before I even opened my eyes. Charging down the stairs with a whole lot of noise, they went right for the front door. Peering out the slit in the curtain, I didn't see a thing except fast moving taillights speeding down the road.

I opened the door slowly with my gun drawn and found a note stuck in my door with a knife that simply said, "Can you feel me coming?"

Sleep didn't come easy after that. I laid there for the next few hours with my now very jumpy boys thinking how much I am not looking forward to a pissing match with the mob.

Friday morning, dead tired from lack of sleep, I dragged my ass to work. Part way through my morning mom called me on her break.

"Missy, did you have any unwanted visitors late last night?"

"You too, huh?"

With a customer in my chair staring at me, I said to mom "We definitely need to talk."

"What do you think if we skip the gym tonight and I meet you at the firing range at 4 o'clock?"

Mom says "Good idea. I think we're going to need it. See you then and Jules, be careful."

"You too."

EPILOG

Later that evening

Sitting in Fritzie's Pub with our wine, we start telling Jack about our midnight visitors and what they left us. He gives us a look of concern and asks "Just what did they leave you"? We tell him about the knives and the note and what the note contained - CAN YOU FEEL ME COMING? And, asked him what do you think?

He says "It sounds like classic Cantone, but how would he know the two of you were involved? (Only the circle knew). This can't be good."

"Well, mom says, "I was thinking about going to the Cape for a few days just to get out of town. What do you think?"

Jack says, "I think it's a great idea."

Jules says "You have the best ideas. A little

R&R, some sun and wine sounds divine."
"When do we leave?"
"As soon as we can get time off from work and get packed."

Jack asks us to say hello to his brother Paulie when we get there.

Another week later

Strolling in the sand with wine in hand, something hits the dock. We both look in shock.
Relax no more. What's in store?

Cantone steams up **HOT SAILS** coming soon!

The second edition in the **SOUL SISTERS** mini mystery series.

NOTE TO OUR READERS:

We hope you enjoyed reading **COLD STORAGE** as much as we enjoyed writing it!

This is the first book in our mini mystery series. It is intended to introduce you to our cast of characters and characters they are.

They make up some of our **Secret Circle**.

JULES–A hairstylist/P.I., partner in Soul Sisters Investigations

ANGEL–Mom/a nurse/P.I. partner in Soul Sisters Investigations, lives at the Cloud

JOE–Dad/construction/also lives at the Cloud

HOMBRE–ex-navy seal/Jules best friend, bounty hunter

NAN–Angel's mom/Jules grandmother/ all around quirky character

VITO–Judge/Sheila's ex-husband/go to guy

SHEILA–Vito's ex-wife/a little crazy

NICK– Investigative reporter

ANDREA–Prosecuting attorney

JACK–Bar tender/Fritzie's Pub/ex-military/go to guy

VINCE–Gym owner/well connected family

CANTONE–Mob Boss, sexy as hell

THE ORIGINAL SECRET CIRCLE SEVEN

Angel
Jules
Ombre
Jack
Nick
Vito
Andrea

OUR INSPIRATION

A favorite doctor for teaching me to not waste a worry.

Annie for keeping me in an endless supply of books.

Barb and Fran for being so good to me over the years.

Nebraska Brace, a nice man, for unknowingly showing us which path to follow in our mission.

Many beautiful sunny days on Cape Cod.